FEARSOME GIANT, FEARLESS CHILD

A Worldwide Jack and the Beanstalk Story

Paul Fleischman

illustrated by

Julie Paschkis

HENRY HOLT AND COMPANY · NEW YORK

In memory of the fearless Dorothy Albee
—P. F.

To Eric and Benjamin Kaye—kind and brave brothers
—J. P.

Henry Holt and Company, *Publishers since 1866*
Henry Holt® is a registered trademark of Macmillan Publishing Group, LLC
175 Fifth Avenue, New York, NY 10010 • mackids.com

Text copyright © 2019 by The Brown-Fleischman Family Trust
Illustrations copyright © 2019 by Julie Paschkis

Library of Congress Control Number: 2018945022
ISBN 978-1-250-15177-3

Our books may be purchased in bulk for promotional, educational, or
business use. Please contact your local bookseller or the Macmillan Corporate
and Premium Sales Department at (800) 221-7945 ext. 5442 or
by e-mail at MacmillanSpecialMarkets@macmillan.com.

First edition, 2019 | Designed by Liz Dresner
The artist used gouache on paper to create these illustrations.
Printed in China by Toppan Leefung Printing Ltd., Dongguan City,
Guangdong Province

1 3 5 7 9 10 8 6 4 2

AUTHOR'S NOTE

Tales of unafraid underdogs give us heart. Their perils are extreme in stories told the world over of a child confronting a man-eating giant or witch. These heroes go by many names, from Jack to Little Thumb to Molly Whuppie. They might have no siblings or be one of many, be average in size or no bigger than a finger. Though they're often scorned for being the youngest and smallest, they're well-armed with cleverness and courage. To get the full account of their exploits, check out surlalunefairytales.com and Margaret Read MacDonald's fine 1993 collection, *Tom Thumb*.

GERMANY

It was scary, but I begged for that story. How the king adored his older children but could barely stand to look at his youngest son.

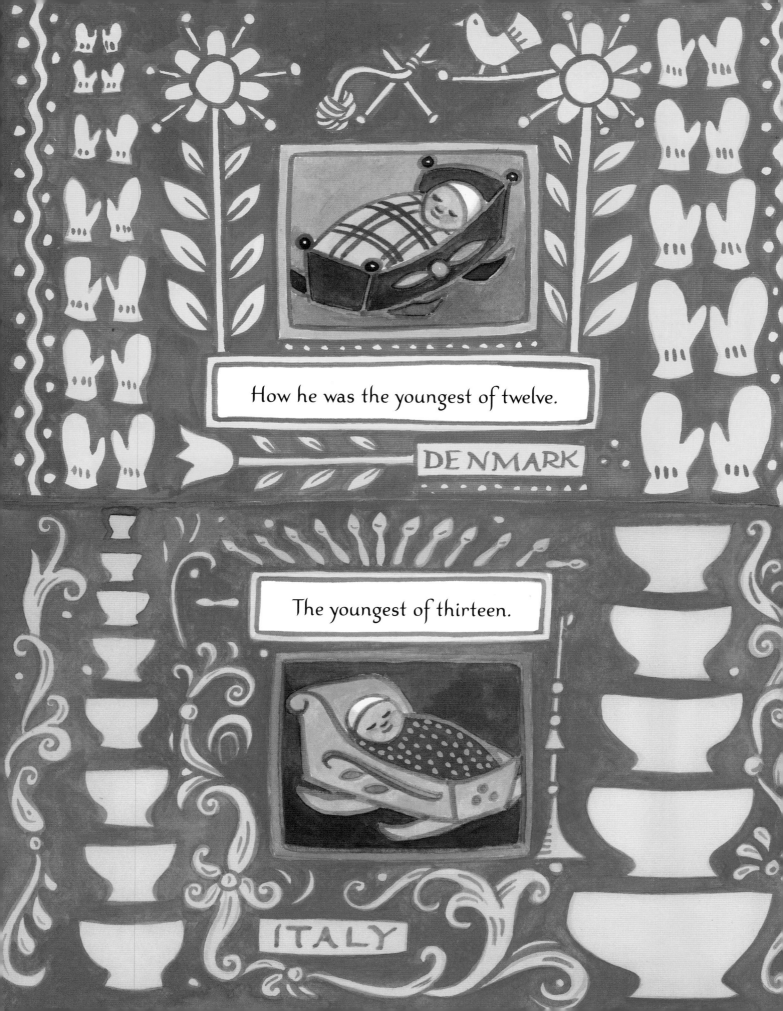

How he was the youngest of twelve.

DENMARK

The youngest of thirteen.

ITALY

How the woman with seven brawny sons gave birth to an eighth who was no bigger than a finger.

ETHIOPIA

The parents were amazed at their inch-long baby.

JAPAN

He was so quiet that everyone took him for stupid. But hungry is what he was, for there wasn't enough food to feed them all. The parents knew something had to be done.

So the father led his son
into the jungle and left him.

INDONESIA

The boy lost his way among the trees. Then, deep in the forest, he spied a palace.

CHILE

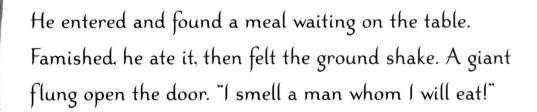

He entered and found a meal waiting on the table.
Famished, he ate it, then felt the ground shake. A giant
flung open the door. "I smell a man whom I will eat!"

PHILIPPINES

"Fee, fi, fo, fum! I smell the
blood of an Englishman!"

ENGLAND

GAMBIA

The brothers lay down to sleep in the witch's house, but the youngest knew that she meant to eat them all. He told his brothers to exchange their white robes for the blue robes worn by the witch's daughters.

Then he switched his brothers' sleeping caps
with the crowns that the ogre's daughters wore.
When the ogre came in the dark of night, it felt
for the caps and killed its own daughters.

FRANCE

GREECE

The little one's brothers were jealous of his cleverness.
They told the king that the boy could do anything,
hoping he'd be given a quest that would end his life.

"Find the princess's thousand pearls scattered in the forest or else you'll be turned to stone."

GERMANY

"Steal the wish-granting jewel that His Majesty keeps in his mouth at night."

MONGOLIA

ETHIOPIA

"Bring me the man-eater's prize bull."

Each time, the boy succeeded. And each time, the king then asked for something new.

DENMARK

ITALY

The lad crept into the monster's house once more, this time to steal his bell-covered pillow. But the moment he touched it, the bells began ringing.

CHILE

The horse began to speak.
"Help! The boy's stealing me!"

The lad watched the golden harp sing a lullaby that put the giant to sleep. He'd already stolen the giant's sacks of gold and his hen that laid golden eggs.

ENGLAND

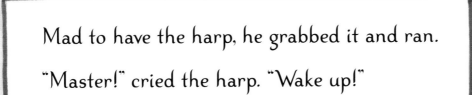

Mad to have the harp, he grabbed it and ran.

"Master!" cried the harp. "Wake up!"

FRANCE

The ogre jumped into his magic boots that let him cover seven leagues at a stride and took off after the brothers.

GAMBIA

The youngest brother heard the witch racing through the forest behind them. Over his shoulder he threw an egg that cracked and became a river blocking her way.

But the witch called her oxen, who
drank up the river. On she raced.

RUSSIA

He heard the Devil galloping on his heels and dropped a piece of gravel into his mule's ear. Quick as lightning the whole country behind him turned into boulders. The Devil had to go back and fetch a gold hammer to crack himself a path—

UNITED STATES

and by that time the lad was long gone.

The witch? She was so mad that she burst into pieces.

DENMARK

MONGOLIA

That speck of a lad? He became king.

NORWAY

The older brothers finally thanked him for saving their lives.

JAPAN

The Lord's daughter made a wish. And suddenly the boy grew to normal size.

Never again was the family hungry.

FRANCE

And everything worked out in the end.
Indeed it did. Now calm yourself, child.
And try to sleep.

United States
of America

Chile